FEET TWO™

Mumble
Saves
the Day!

by Judy Katschke
illustrated by Mark Sexton

Mumble was famous for his happy feet, but on this particular day, he wasn't very happy. Erik, his son, had wandered away from Emperor Land to the land of the Adelies with his two best friends, Bo and Atticus. When Mumble found the fluffy trio, it was time to go back home.

The last place Erik wanted to go was back to Emperor Land.
He couldn't dance like his dad or the other penguins.

"I don't belong there," Erik sighed. If only he could be just
like his hero, the Mighty Sven. If only he could *fly*!

Just as the penguins were halfway home, the
icy ground beneath their feet trembled, followed
by an earsplitting *CRAAAAAACK*!
   It was an earthquake!

"Uncle Mumble, are we okay?" Atticus asked after the shaking stopped.

"Let's keep moving," Mumble said. Then he saw something blocking their path. It was a crevasse – a deep, dark crack in the ice. How would they get home now?

"We'll just have to go all the way around," Mumble declared.

"Why not go over *that*?" Bo asked. She pointed to a narrow bridge of ice. "Shortcuts are always shorter."

Mumble looked at the ice bridge and frowned. The crossing may have been shorter – but it sure wasn't *safer*!

"This way is better," Mumble said, pointing to the long way around. But when Mumble turned, the kids weren't following him. They were crossing the dangerous ice bridge!

"Kids! STOP!" Mumble shouted.

Bo and Atticus obeyed Mumble, but Erik did not.

Mumble had to stop Erik from going any farther. He shuffled across the narrow bridge to catch up to Erik, Bo and Atticus. Suddenly . . .

"G'day, sport!" a voice called.

Looking up, the penguins couldn't believe their eyes. It was the most enormous Elephant seal they had ever seen!

Mumble tried to stay cool. "If you don't mind backing up a little bit," he told the seal, "we'll just squeeze past."

"The Beachmaster backs up for nobody!" replied the creature.

Mumble tried to reason with the Beachmaster. He had to get the kids safely to the other side of the bridge. But the seal refused to move.

Bo decided to take action. She hopped on the Beachmaster's nose and backflipped over him. Then – *WHACK!* – the seal flipped his gigantic tail and sent her flying. She landed in the snow right where she had started! Still, the seal refused to move.

The kids would not give up. Atticus slapped the Beachmaster's trunk, but a blast of wind from the huge trunk knocked him off his feet. Then Erik stepped up to the bully. The Beachmaster sucked him up with his trunk and spit him out, tossing Erik backward over his head!

Mumble desperately needed to get to Erik's side and shouted at the beast, "GET OUT OF MY WAY!" With a rumbling roar, the Beachmaster reared his gigantic body and crashed down on the icy bridge. Then – *CRUUUUUUNCH!* – the ice under the Beachmaster shattered. The penguins watched as the bridge suddenly disappeared into the crevasse, taking the Beachmaster with it.

Looking across the crevasse, Mumble froze. Erik was standing on the other side. But he wasn't alone. Next to him were two baby Elephant seals — and they wanted their dad!

Mumble was worried about Erik, but the baby seals needed help, too. He peered over the edge and saw the Beachmaster clinging to a ledge. If the seal lost his grip, he would plummet down hundreds of metres.

"Can you move?" asked Mumble. "Can you pull yourself up?"
The Beachmaster tried to move. Then, with a deafening
CREEEEAK, the entire ledge gave way and the seal plunged out
of sight into the deep, dark crevasse.

The penguins and baby seals peered way down below into the darkness. They could just make out the massive bulk of the Beachmaster – squeezed between the walls of ice.

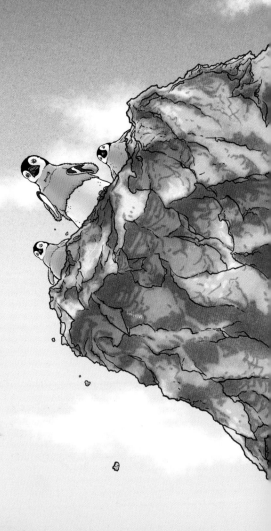

The Beachmaster thought he was a goner stuck at the bottom
of this deep ice cave, but Mumble refused to give up.

"What can *he* do?" one of the seal pups asked, looking at
Erik. "He's just an ordinary penguin!"

Mumble hurried to the sea nearby and jumped into the water. He was careful not to wake a Leopard seal sleeping on an ice floe close by. From the water below, he saw the Beachmaster resting on a thick sheet of ice. Swimming at it, he tried to crack through the wall of the cave to set the seal free, but it wouldn't break.

Mumble refused to give up. He paddled over to the Leopard seal, still dozing on the floating ice pad, and shouted at him to get his attention.

"Hey you, dufus!" he said.

The sleeping seal was suddenly wide awake and plunged into the water after Mumble. Mumble swam fast, fancy spirals as the seal chased him.

When Mumble reached the cave where the Beachmaster was trapped,
he slowed down and waited until the seal closed in on him. The Leopard
seal bared his sharp teeth as he opened his mouth wide – but before he
could chomp down, Mumble zipped to the side.

SLAM! The seal plowed into the frozen wall and came face-to-face with the Beachmaster. The Leopard seal gulped at the sight of the enormous beast and shot off.

Water gushed into the cave through the crack the Leopard seal had made, and the Beachmaster floated safely to the top of the crevasse.

All the penguins were happily reunited, and the beaming Beachmaster was back with his kids.

"I owe you one, my friend," the Beachmaster promised Mumble. "All you have to do is ask."

Mumble said goodbye to his enormous, new friend. He didn't know what that favour would someday be, but he had a feeling it would be a BIG one!

As the penguins started their long trek back to Emperor Land, Mumble turned to Erik, Bo and Atticus with a smile. "I don't know about you," he said. "But I can't wait to get home."

Erik couldn't wait, either. After all, he had a new hero, and this time it wasn't the incredible flying Sven.

This time, it was *his dad*!